A New Magically Mysterious Adventure by

GLORIA ESTEFAN

Noelle's Treasure Tale

illustrated by MICHAEL GARLAND

rayo

An Imprint of HarperCollinsPublishers

The dark skies seemed to open, pouring rivers of rain
as eleven brave galleons made their way back to Spain.
They were loaded with treasure, gold and silver doubloons,
thunder sounding the way on a night with no moon.
The wind tossed them and turned them. Their fate was quite plain.
They were all going down in a great hurricane.

It was storming outside as the little girl read,
and Noelle got so scared she hid under the bed.
"Let me read you the part about pirates and ghosts
and the reason they call it the Great Treasure Coast."
But Noelle thought she'd heard waaaay too much information.
They were going *right there, the next day,* on vacation!

"Maybe *we'll* find the treasure, Noelle, some for each.
There's a chance that it might have washed up on the beach.
If the stories are true, one piece never found
was the Christmas gift meant for the Queen, a gold crown!"

Noelle's head was spinning while hatching a plan.
She'd have to dig *zillions* of holes in the sand!
If there was a treasure, by golly, she'd find it,
and maybe unravel the mystery behind it.

When they got there, the two of them raced to the beach
as a gull seemed to welcome them both with a screech.
Then Noelle, with excitement too hard to control,
started digging away when she found a small hole.
Noelle scooped out sand till her snout could fit in,
and then yelped as she felt a sharp pain on her chin.
She flung her head back, and a creature with claws
yelled and screamed as he hung there, attached to her jaw.

"STOP, STOP, STOP what you're doing, insensitive hound!
You're a dog! There's no way you can live underground!"
"I was digging for treasure I was told might be here.
Didn't mean to upset you," said Noelle, quite sincere.
"Listen up!" said the crab. "I've been searching forever.
We might find it much faster if we both work together."

Farther down on the beach Noelle saw, in a bunch,
twenty sandpipers slurping up sand fleas for lunch.
They were miniature birds running fast to and fro,
trying not to get caught in the waves' undertow.
One called out to Noelle, "We don't mean to butt in,
but if treasure's your goal, in the forest begin."

Noelle crouched down and asked, "Want to go for a ride?"
The crab climbed on her back and they ventured inside.

Glaring under some brush like two marbles they shone,
eyes that stared at Noelle like a dog at a bone.
Then a deep, grumbly voice broke the still of the air.
"Whose permission have *you* to just traipse through my lair?"

"What's your name?" asked Noelle of the big, fearsome cat.
"My name's Bob," he replied. "Want to stop for a chat?"
"I'm afraid we must go and continue our quest.
We're in search of a treasure. Any place you'd suggest?"

"I suggest you take cover," the wise bobcat purred.
"There's a hurricane coming! Or haven't you heard?"
"Then we'd better get going!" Noelle said with worry.
"We'll have to head back to the house in a hurry!"

They discovered a path and decided to follow.
But the rain made them hide in a log, big and hollow.
Noelle thought out loud, "What we need is a map.
But until it stops raining, we might as well nap."

As Noelle nodded off, she could hear distant thunder
while dreaming of treasure and pirates who plunder. . . .

She was on a big ship being bounced side to side.
Waves, like mountains of water, crashed and landed inside.
At the helm was a seagull. Like a statue he stood,
with a patch on one eye and a leg made of wood.
He was shouting out orders. Noelle's heart quickly sank.
"This dog's after me treasure! She must now walk the plank!"

Noelle felt a sharp sword poke her right in the back.
A raccoon wearing boots had her under attack.
"Move along, scurvy dog, or I'll slice you in three."
Noelle took a deep breath and jumped into the sea.

Just as soon as Noelle was convinced she would drown,
she discovered she was falling "up" and not down.
On the back of a turtle who had swum down to save her,
to the surface she rode on her "turt-el-evator."
She said, "How can I ever your kindness repay?
I will give *you* the treasure if I find it one day."

The great sea turtle said, "I know just where it lies.
I will whisper some clues that you must memorize."
So Noelle listened well but then wanted to scream
when she woke up to find IT HAD ALL BEEN A DREAM!

Her incredible dream to the crab she confided,
as she told him each clue that the turtle provided.
"At the edge of the forest find the tree with the heart.
Count twelve paces due east; it is there you will start.
From that point you will see, fifty yards to the north,
several mounds in the sand, but your aim is the fourth.
It is marked with a stick with a number and date.
You must get there by dark, or it might be too late."

Noelle's heart beat faster with each clue that they found.
All at once there it was, the mysterious mound!
And just as Noelle thought her journey complete,
something wiggly and jiggly shook under her feet.

Little heads, tiny flippers crawled out of the sand
on their way to the ocean as if on command.
Baby turtles, one hundred, scooted fast past Noelle.
Some took off the wrong way; one flipped back on its shell.

Then a hungry raccoon and a ravenous snake
showed up, out of nowhere, for sea turtle steak.
But Noelle, thinking fast, out of pure intuition,
stood like stone in their path, knowing this was her mission;
growled a growl that was frightful, then chased them away.
And each baby sea turtle she then led the right way.

Far from shore a huge turtle, like the one she had dreamed,
waved a flipper in thanks, at least that's how it seemed.
Noelle figured her dream must have come as a sign.
She glanced back at the mound, where she saw something shine.
"One more turtle!" she cried. "We must dig farther down!"
Gently using her teeth, she pulled out a gold crown!

To the day, one year later, in a palace in Spain,
the King toasted Noelle with a glass of champagne.
"I declare that Noelle has a worth we can't measure
for returning to Spain our historical treasure."

The little girl hugged her and said, "I'm so proud!"
Then a "HIP HIP HOORAY!" burst from out of the crowd.
Noelle thought to herself, though gold may bring pleasure,
she had learned from the turtles, LIFE IS the *true* treasure.

To Emily, Nayib, and everyone who loves animals

CD Credits
See with Your Heart
Lead Vocals: Gloria Estefan. Music: Emilio Estefan. Lyrics: Gloria M. Estefan.
Produced by: Emilio Estefan. Musical Arrangements: Marco Linares. Colombian
Tiple: Luz Angela Jimenez. Guitars, Bass, Drum Programming, Keyboards: Marco
Linares. Percussion: Alberto Vargas. Additional Percussion: Emilio Estefan.
Background Vocals: Yisel Duque and Luz Angela Jimenez. Additional Background
Vocals: Marco Linares. Tracking Engineers: Alfred Figueroa, Jose "Che" Colon, Jaron
Bozeman. Mixing Engineer: Alfred Figueroa. Assistant Engineer: Ryan Wolff.
Recorded and Mixed at: Crescent Moon Studios, Miami, FL. Published by: Foreign
Imported Productions & Publishing, Inc. (BMI). ℗ and © 2006 Estefan Enterprises, Inc.
Manufactured by HarperCollins Publishers,
10 East 53rd Street, New York, NY 10022
WARNING: All rights reserved.
Unauthorized duplication is a violation of applicable laws.

NOELLE'S TREASURE TALE: *A New Magically Mysterious Adventure*
Copyright © 2006 by Estefan Enterprises, Inc.
All rights reserved. Manufactured in China.
No part of this book may be used or reproduced in any manner whatsoever
without written permission except in the case of brief quotations embodied in
critical articles and reviews. For information address HarperCollins Publishers Inc.,
10 East 53rd Street, New York, NY 10022.
HarperCollins books may be purchased for educational, business,
or sales promotional use. For information please write:
Special Markets Department, HarperCollins Publishers Inc.,
10 East 53rd Street, New York, NY 10022.
First Rayo edition published 2006.
Library of Congress Cataloging-in-Publication Data is available.
ISBN-10: 0-06-112614-4 (English) – ISBN-13: 978-0-06-112614-7 (English)
ISBN-10: 0-06-112616-0 (Spanish) – ISBN-13: 978-0-06-112616-1 (Spanish)
06 07 08 09   10 9 8 7 6 5 4 3 2 1